Lucius Artorius Castus

DE BELLO LEMURES

Or,
The Roman War Against
the Zombies of Armorica

ANNOTATED AND WITH AN
INTRODUCTION BY THOMAS BROOKSIDE

HISTORIC Ω CLASSICS

Set in Monotype Georgia

10 9 8 7 6 5 4 3 2

To Thomas Erasmus

FOREWORD

At the close of the last century, the revolutionary advances in the imaging of ancient manuscripts achieved by the team assembled by Baltimore's Walters Art Museum to recover the *Archimedes Codex C* ushered in a new era in paleography.[1] Documents that had been believed to be irretrievably illegible due to the ravages of time, dirt, weather, vandalism, and even volcanic eruption were now decipherable using the team's cutting-edge multispectral imaging and synchrotronic x-ray techniques. New technology made it possible to imagine that "lost" works by ancient playwrights, essayists, scientists and mathematicians might be rediscovered hiding in virtually any repository of ancient or medieval documents, and researchers swarmed through libraries and museum collections to seek them out.

---

[1] The study and scholarly interpretation of ancient documents and systems of writing.

Although the techniques in question were of great value in uncovering text obscured by water damage or carbonization, their greatest utility was in assisting the reading and deciphering of palimpsests.[1] Even the most faint and obscure writing could be thrown into vivid relief by multispectral imaging of the materials used in different ink types. In the case of the *Archimedes Codex C*, although the original ink had been scraped off the pages with a pumice stone and the writing surface cleaned with acid by the 13th century monk who re-used the parchment to make a prayer book, researchers armed with the new technology were able to see past the monk's handwriting to the Archimedes text below it. As the technique was refined, even multiple palimpsests – where the erasing and overwriting process had happened more than once – yielded up their secrets.

It was perhaps inevitable that this process would lead to the discovery of so-called *secret palimpsests* [or "Yetis", as they are sometimes jokingly named in the paleography community]: documents which had not previously even been identifiable as palimpsests because the original handwriting had been so thoroughly erased that it was no longer visible to the naked eye, or even under an ultraviolet lamp. After Oxford researchers discovered the first "Yeti", literally

---

[1] Parchment or other writing material re-used after earlier writing has been erased.

every ancient or medieval document had to be considered a potential palimpsest, and the amount of material that could be usefully subjected to analysis as part of the search for lost works expanded by several orders of magnitude.

It was during a comprehensive multi-spectral search of the document trove held at the Universitätsbibliothek Salzburg that the curious and much-debated work that follows was discovered. A contemporary copy of Freidank's *Bescheidenheit* that had not previously been identified as a palimpsest was revealed to be a "Yeti" by synchrotronic x-ray analysis. The Freidank copy had been assembled out of a pastiche of parchments from different documents. A portion of the underlying text was quickly determined to be a fragment of Vitruvius' *On Architecture*; the balance, it eventually became clear, was something else indeed.

Lucius Artorius Castus was a minor figure in 2nd century history, known primarily from inscriptions, including his funerary inscription. Despite his personal obscurity [some might say insignificance], Castus is relatively well-known in the modern era, due mainly to the fact that his *nomen*[1] and some details of his life history

---

[1] The *nomen* was the second name under the Roman naming convention and was generally the name of the

and legionary cavalry service in Roman Britannia have caused him to be advanced as a candidate to have been the historical basis for the "Arthur" legend. When it was recognized that the new work purported to be a copy of a history written by Castus in the form of a long letter or address, delighted scholars hoped that it might shed light on this curiously interesting figure, as well as upon the broader history of the declining years of the Antonine dynasty. As the complete – or nearly complete – work was uncovered, that initial hope and delight turned into shock, and furious controversy.

The controversy, of course, arose from the fact that the letter purported to be an account of a *supernatural event* - or an epidemiological event so badly misunderstood as to appear supernatural - involving Roman legionaries and auxiliaries on the Brittany peninsula in the late 2nd century.

Immediately, accusations were leveled that the work was a forgery or hoax, but it was rapidly determined that this was virtually impossible. The chain of provenance of the Salzburg Freidank was beyond question, and that undisputed 13th century work was written *over* the Castus text. If *De Bello Lemures*, as

---

family or *gens*. "Artorius" was a minor *gens* and Lucius was its only known member to serve in Britannia.

the work became known,[1] is a hoax, it has to be a 13th century hoax – and the questions that would be raised if that were so would be almost as profound as those raised if the work is a genuine recounting of the experiences or perceived experiences of a 2nd century Roman nobleman. In the production of this translation I have worked with the assumption that the work is genuine.

Others have argued that, given the subject matter, it is plain that the work was intended to be a work of fiction or proto-novel after the manner of the *Satyricon*. This is, of course, a position that has in its favor the fact that it does not require us to explain the bizarre events the author describes. But this view is undermined by the fact that the type of narrative contained in *De Bello Lemures* was only attained elsewhere by Roman authors in the production of histories; as a proto-novel it would represent an advance in literary form, achieved just once for this work and never achieved again by any Roman author. In addition, the work would not merely be a literary advance as a proto-novel; it would represent a proto-novel written as a *faux* history, ess-

[1] Castus, naturally, did not give his letter a title; the title is a later addition by an unknown medieval copyist. The date of the title's addition is not known, but the ungrammatical, bowdlerized Latin argues for a post-Carolingian timeframe.

entially leaping over the entire early history of the form and landing squarely in the middle of post-modernism. The proto-novel theory is also undermined by the fact that we have absolutely no evidence that Castus was a literary figure in addition to being a military one – no literary activity is mentioned in the inscription on his funerary monument, and no fragment of his writing or reference to his writing appears in the work of any other Roman author. To support the proto-novel thesis we would have to conclude that Castus was a unique literary figure who produced a unique literary work; and that despite this work being completely unnoticed by his contemporaries it was preserved by copyists for a thousand years before it was finally forgotten. Next to this string of unlikelihoods, the idea that *De Bello Lemures* is exactly what it claims to be is not that incredible.

Archaeological research at sites referenced by Castus is ongoing. It is greatly aided by the precise description of locations and distances the author provides in his narrative. We may be just one turn of the spade and one more "discovery" away from settling the question of which camp in the debate over this work is correct. Until the question is settled, we have to be satisfied with the work itself.

A Note on Punctuation:

All punctuation used here is interpolated from the text. Classical Latin did not employ punctuation. In some cases, to aid the readability of the text and for aesthetic purposes conversations Castus recounts in the third person have been re-arranged into the dialogue form, including conversation marks, that is customary and familiar to modern readers.

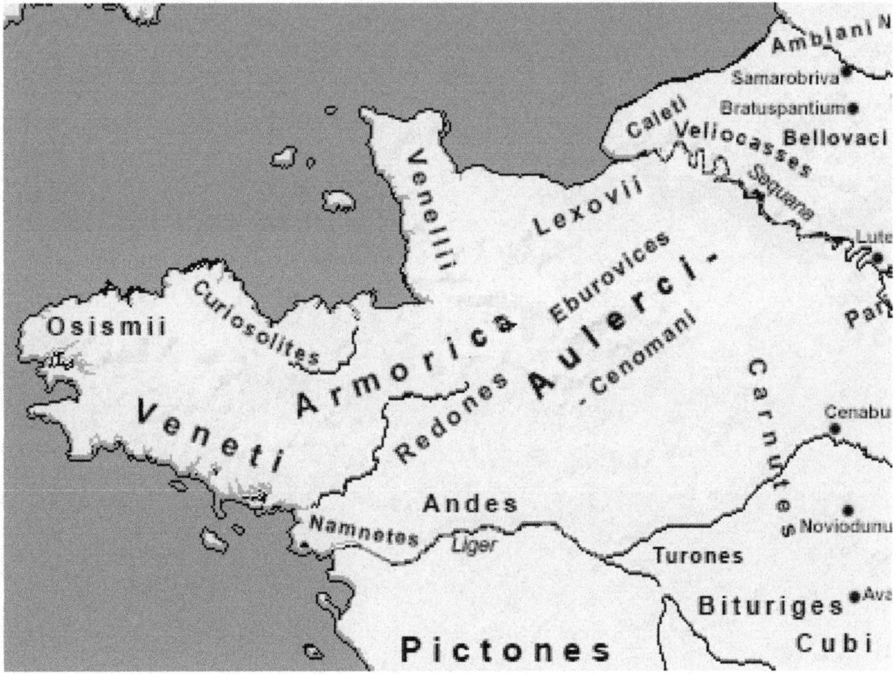
Ambiani
Samarobriva
Bratuspantium
Caleti
Veliocasses
Bellovaci
Sequana
Venellii
Lexovii
Osismii
Curiosolites
Armorica
Eburovices
Aulerci
Cenomani
Redones
Veneti
Carnutes
Andes
Namnetes
Liger
Turones
Bituriges
Cubi
Pictones

ONE

In the year when Marcus Umbrius Primus was *consul suffectus*[1] the deserter and traitor Maternus,[2] drawing to himself the worst criminals and desperadoes, launched his revolt in that portion of Gallia Comata[3] called Armorica.

Armorica consisted of a broad peninsula, extending a considerable distance out into Oceanus, along with the land watered by the river Liger[4] and its tributaries. Although included in the province of Gallia Lugdunensis, it has long been a backwater, with many of its villages

---

[1] 185 CE.
[2] Confirmed by Herodian's account of the conspiracy of Maternus in his *History of the Roman Empire since the Death of Marcus Aurelius*.
[3] "Long-haired" Gaul.
[4] The Loire River.

as rude as they were when the great Julius first brought our civilization to the northern Gauls. The long traffic and commerce between the Armoricans and the tribes of Britannia, including the savage Selgovae and Caledonii beyond our defenses, is no doubt responsible for this backwardness.[1]

Maternus preyed upon the simplicity of the Armoricans, gaining their allegiance with false promises and deceptions. He took great advantage of the resentment of the peasant for the tax collector, as brigands of his kind always do. In each city his men freed all the prisoners, no matter how degenerate their crimes, and promised these men freedom in exchange for service;[2] this same offer was made to many slaves. He also cruelly played upon the superstitions prevalent among the tribes of the peninsula, which the governors at Lugdunum[3] have never been able to fully stamp out. His promises to restore the ancient religion of the grove won many of the uncouth to his side, and brought many secret Druids out of hiding.

---

[1] Castus' previous posting with legion VI Victrix took him to Bremetennacum near Hadrian's Wall.

[2] Herodian uses virtually identical language to describe Maternus' recruitment of criminals, raising the possibility that he employed Castus as a direct source.

[3] Lyons.

I, Lucius Artorius Castus, was made *dux*[1] of the cohorts sent by the Emperor to crush these bandits and to restore the writ of law. Crossing from Dubris to Gesoriacum[2] with my Iazyges[3] and with such cohorts of the VI Victrix as could be spared from duty at Eboracum,[4] I rapidly drove Maternus and his lieutenants into hiding,[5] and snuffed out the revolt as water will a flame.

It is not necessary for me to recount that campaign in any great detail here, as it has been exhaustively recorded in my letters to Publius Helvius Pertinax,[6] copies of which were read to the Senate. I mean instead, in this letter, to describe the strange and horrible events that followed the revolt, after the last open defiance had been defeated in the field and those survivors who had not been captured and executed had melted away into the countryside. For in Arm-

---

[1] A generalship of two or more legions, alt. over all troops in a province; later "Duke".

[2] Roughly from Dover to the Pas de Calais.

[3] Sarmatian or Scythian tribesmen who settled in Britain under Roman officers following the Balkan wars of Marcus Aurelius.

[4] York.

[5] Herodian reports that Maternus, after fleeing Gaul, traveled to Rome and attempted to assassinate the emperor Commodus. At the time this letter was composed, that event was still in the future, and from Castus' perspective the revolt appeared over.

[6] Governor of Britannia at the end of Castus' tour there and later emperor.

orica I met a greater enemy than any bandit chief or usurper. A horror stalks the forests there that cannot be propitiated, and this history must be heeded if it is not to devour us all.

TWO

We crucified the last of the rebel die-hards on a hill overlooking the thirteenth milestone outside of Portus Namnetus[1] on the eve of the Kalends of November.[2] They had been captured by ruse the day before, as they raided a nearby villa. Short of food and maddened by shame at our many victories over them, their foraging could no longer be distinguished from rapine, and their desperation made them careless. I had ordered lightly armed scouts and javelin-men from the provincial auxiliaries hidden among the farm outbuildings and in the *ergastulum*[3] of the estate, and these had sprung forth when the raiders arrived; they fixed the enemy in place until cavalry hidden nearby could engage and capture them. We had piled the dead into an open offal midden

---

[1] Nantes.
[2] The *Kalends* was the 1st of the month, so this date would correspond to October 31st.
[3] Partially underground slave quarters or prison.

and marched the prisoners to a site where their horrible end could be instructive to the passers-by.

The crucifixions were just a last bit of business to attend to prior to closing out the campaign. Each *palus*[1] had been set to face as many of the others as possible, so that the rebels could all see the end to which their crimes had brought them and their fellows. I wished to conclude the executions that afternoon, in order to return my men on the following day to the main encampment outside the port; as the prisoners hung in the bronze autumn sun, we waited and fretted, impatient to leave. To speed matters along I had ordered that the *crurifragium*[2] be performed; the executioner's boys had gone to each gibbet in turn and broken the condemned man's legs with a heavy iron bar, to hasten the moment at which their strength and breath would fail. This would save us much time, even if it was a mercy that the rebels did not deserve; a man with his legs intact can survive on the cross for days, but

[1] Crucifixions were sometimes conducted by suspending the victim from a single upright post with no crossbeam called a *palus*. Despite the absence of a crosspiece the *palus* was still commonly referred to as a cross.

[2] Much debate has traditionally surrounded whether the *crurifragium* was designed to worsen or temper the punishment of the condemned. Castus' report seems to support the latter argument.

without the ability to support his weight a prisoner will expire quite quickly.

With me was Radamyntos, the decurion of the senior *turma*[1] of the Iazyges contingent, along with a group of local notables led by Gaius Iulius Rufus, called Rufus, the region's major landlord. Radamyntos and his countrymen were nearly as great a spectacle for the Armoricans as the punishment of the rebels; although they were a common sight on the frontier, no men of their race had ever penetrated this deep into the northwestern countryside of Gaul, and their odd appearance and kit drew much attention. Although I was in standard undress uniform, wearing merely my *paludamentum*[2] and belt, Radamyntos was in full armor even for this light duty, as was his custom. The citizens and the *peregrini*[3] freely gaped at him. The Iazyges wear long-sleeved tunics of mail that extend

---

[1] A *turma* was a cavalry unit of approx. 30 men. Thus Radamyntos' position roughly corresponds to the *primus pilus* centurion of an infantry legion.

[2] A command officer's cloak; a variation on the common soldier's *sagum*.

[3] A *peregrinus* was a free provincial subject of the empire who did not hold Roman citizenship. Prior to the widespread enfranchisement undertaken by Caracalla in 212 AD, a large majority of the inhabitants of the empire were *peregrini*. These provincials enjoyed fewer rights at law than Roman citizens, but they were present among all economic classes; it is unclear for this reason whether Castus means to refer to the peasants present, or some fraction of the landlords.

down to the knee, and their sturdy conical helmets have iron nose guards that cover most of their faces. They drape their horses in thick leather set with bronze scales, and carry a heavy spear they call a *contus*.[1] Radamyntos wore a belt to spread the weight of his mail: a golden hedgehog with unpolished gems for eyes, roughly crafted in a crude manner that accentuated his barbaric origins. Rufus, who had no military background at all, was properly intimidated, and he could barely contain his own trembling at the sight.

The prisoners' wailing, loud and desperate in its pleading at first, quickly trailed off to whimpering an hour or so after the *crurifragium*. One by one, their voices fell silent. When only a few were left, some of the witnesses began to bet on which prisoner would last the longest, and the air was filled with the calls familiar at any horse race or at thanksgiving games. This greatly distressed Rufus, who did not even attempt to conceal his disapproving frowns and sighs. The landlord's obvious discomfort brought to the face of Radamyntos the bare, tight-lipped smile that is the substitute for great laughter among those of his tribe. Thinking that I might trick him into making an unguarded statement in sympathy with Maternus, I asked

[1] Castus' description supports the argument that the Sarmatians had by this point in history begun using the true heavy lance, later to be copied by the Sassanid and Roman / Byzantine cataphracts.

Rufus for the source of his disquiet. He gave nothing away, but merely replied, "*Dux*, it grieves me to hear the catcalls of the crowd directed at men hanging on the cross, even such scum as these." This struck me as very softhearted, and not a very good reflection on his class, but I could detect nothing politically objectionable in it.

At length, as the sun drew low, only two prisoners survived: one of Maternus' fellow deserters from the legions, a great brute with a square head, and a shriveled old man with spots on his bald pate and the look of boiled leather. This looked to be no contest, and nearly all present expected the legionary to be the last. It surprised us all when his death rattle came just as twilight began to creep down the hillside. Those few who bet on the old man did not have long to cheer or gloat, though, for as soon as he realized he was now without his fellows, his face took on a look of great determination, and he began to declaim in a strange tongue, in a strong and piercing voice that was scarcely to be believed possible from one as frail as he at the end of a terrible punishment.

At the sound of that voice Rufus and his fellow landlords, as well as those peasants whose curiosity had drawn them near, blanched with fear. Many of them made obscene hand-gestures or clutched at some *fascinum*[1] on their their person, as if to ward off the evil eye. Some seemed to recognize the strange speech and the particular curse or spell, while some seemed to suffer a more general fear. Certainly the Iazyges did not need to understand the words to recognize a curse when they heard one; they held their formation, but muttered to one another. I thought to call for a ladder and tongs, so that the man's tongue might be struck out, but before I could do so his voice rose to one last great height and then was stilled. His head bobbed about and then hung down on his spindly neck.

After an interval where all stood still, disturbed and hushed in the half-light, I asked if anyone present had understood the dying man's words. Rufus spoke up, with great reluctance.

"*Dux*..." he said, "...the old one was one of those who claimed to be one of the hidden college of druids. Whether he truly was, or merely pretended to be in order to spread fear and to gain a position among the traitors, I cannot say. But in the language of the country, he declared that we were impious to dare to slay him at the beginning of *Samonios*." Before they adopted our civilized calendar, the Gauls celebrated their new year at this time, and also

---

[1] A token or protective charm, usually in the shape of a phallus.

a festival honoring their ancestors and begging favors of the dead.[1] "He says that since we have killed him, he will return and lead the vengeful dead against us."

Many who were present shuddered to hear this, and held their charms fast yet again. But Radamyntos did not, and I did not. Radamyntos considered that living enemies were better to be feared than dead ones, and I – I, to my regret, thought that the old man was a charlatan or a fool.

His charge of impiety was correct. My respect for the gods has long been a matter of my duty to the state, and has never been truly rooted in my breast. I have always given the gods their bare due, but not more; and I have never feared them. In my pride I laughed at the old man's curse thus explained, and showed his corpse my back.

---

[1] Better known to moderns as the festival of Samhain, the pagan antecedent to All Hallows' Eve or Halloween.

THREE

Our soldiers I sent back to their marching-camp at the tenth milestone, where they joined the two *cohors peditata*[1] and one *cohors alaria*[2] who had not already been sent on to Lutetia[3] following the defeat of the main body of our enemies.

Radamyntos and a tribune, Aulus Furius Pacilus, called Pacilus, accompanied me to the nearby estate of Rufus. Pacilus was not well known to me; he was attached for service to one of the legions of the Rhine frontier, and had been lent to me for the space of this campaign. He was said to be an eloquent dinner-companion, however, and I brought

---

[1] Cohort of foot, i.e. infantry. A cohort consisted of approximately 500 men.
[2] Allied or auxiliary cohort – in this context undoubtedly the remaining Sarmatian cavalry.
[3] Paris.

him with me on this occasion to improve our acquaintance.[1]

The land near the road was heavily wooded, with the forests broken only intermittently by clearings for the small tenant farms. Rufus did not directly work his land with the large slave gangs common in areas of heavier settlement, and he did not have more than a modest *villa rustica*.[2] There were many more of the clearings on the south side of the road, where the land sloped down to the river, than on the north, where the land was waste. Rufus surprised me by riding with us; I did not expect that of one as unmilitary as he.[3]

The villa was not a large one for such a substantial landowner, nor was it very sump-

---

[1] There is some debate as to whether accepting hospitality from Rufus in this way and not returning directly to the camp could be considered dereliction of duty. There are few other examples of this so minutely recorded, and it is hard to determine what the expectations for a commander in this type of campaign situation would have been. There is also lively debate about whether Radamyntos attended in the role of bodyguard or guest. His rank and "foreign" status argue for the former, but Castus' general attitude towards him is ambiguous in the early part of the text.

[2] The portion of a rural villa devoted to the production of foodstuffs for the maintenance of the landowner's household. These could be quite extensive, as many landlords aspired to self-sufficiency on their estates.

[3] The Roman saddle was quite primitive, and lacked stirrups. Most civilians preferred to avoid riding and to travel by cart or sedan chair.

tuous. It was only a few *stadia*[1] from the road, on top of a low rise. The river below came into view as we climbed; a dark vein in the grey twilight. As we approached the door, I saw that Rufus had no *janitor*[2] and kept his own key. The house was very simple: it had no atrium, but had a single corridor that ran from the front door to the back, lined with doors that led to the bedrooms, kitchen, and study. It was the kind of sturdy, unpretentious farmhouse one can find throughout the hinterland of Britannia and Gaul.[3] Servants greeted the master of the house when we entered, but no great number of them; this, perhaps, explained why Rufus did not travel by bearer.

I wondered if Rufus was something of a miser. Although only marginally prosperous, the area had several estates more luxurious than his, and many men owned large numbers of agricultural slaves. For one of the major landowners of the region to live so humbly, and to refrain from using slaves to increase the yield of his estate, was incongruous.

---

[1] Each *stadium* was approximately 185 meters.

[2] A slave was often symbolically chained in the doorway of a Roman home to serve as a doorman and watchman.

[3] Attempts to locate the villa described here have not been successful. From Castus' description, it seems to be quite similar to that excavated at Lockleys, Welwyn. See Blair, 125.

In the *triclinium*[1] after we had doffed our cloaks and washed our hands an aged and lame slave served us bread and soft cheese from the estate, along with some eggs and greens, and wine without too much water. Had I known how my night was to proceed, I would have eaten more and drunk less.

As we dined, Rufus made general conversation about the local hardships brought on by the late disturbances, and made polite inquiries about the conditions on the frontiers in Germania and Britannia. I possess no great facility for dinner-chatter, but Pacilus deserved his reputation; he was favored by an urbane polish that his time on the frontiers had not yet worn away. I let the tribune satisfy our host's curiosity in the main. As I idled on the *lectus*,[2] half listening and half absorbed in my own thoughts, I noticed an oddity: the floor mosaic - a depiction of the abduction of Europa by Zeus in the guise of a white bull, which was quite fine, compared to the rest of the dwelling – was largely covered over by rushes. Had the rushes been fresh and full, and not dried to a thin brown by the heat passed to the floor by the

---

[1] The traditional Roman dining area.
[2] The older style of Roman dining couch.

hypocaust,[1] the mosaic might have been totally obscured.

When I asked Rufus for the purpose of the rushes, imagining it to be some custom of Armorica, he informed me that he found the mosaic disturbing; but that he did not have the heart to remove it, as it had been a favorite of his father. I let the strangeness of this pass without comment; I am fortunate enough that I become more courteous, and not less, with wine.

Pacilus would have lingered after the apples,[2] but I was in no mood for *comissatio*.[3] The road and the campaign had set an ache in my bones, and Rufus did not strike me as the right host for such an event in any case. Instead, I called for my sandals[4] and gave our host the type of gracious but impersonal thanks one gives to a provincial one will likely never see again.

The darkness was advanced when we departed, as it was now several hours after sun-down and there was only the merest sliver of

---

[1] The hypocaust was a central heating system; heat from a fire tended by servants passed through vents under the floors, heating the rooms above.
[2] An idiomatic expression meaning "after dessert", which was not necessarily apples.
[3] A drinking bout accompanied by baudy or boisterous conversation.
[4] Latin *soleas poscere:* another idiomatic expression, describing making preparations to leave.

new moon. Rufus lent us one of his farm-boys to carry torches to help lead us back to the road. The night had cooled rapidly, as it will in the northern autumn, and the Archer hung over us in a cloudless and clear sky. The torches lit the breath of our mounts, as we carefully walked them back to the road, but not much else.

Pacilus walked near me, and we talked in low tones. He voiced the opinion that our recent host was a follower of Christus. This suspicion, he related, had grown all through our supper, and he had concealed it from all present only with difficulty. He gave as his evidence the disquiet the man had shown at the crucifixion of the rebels. The Christians, he explained, identify the cross with their god, and are jealous of its application to mere criminals. This also accounted for the rushes that obscured the mosaic; since the Christians were a type of Jew, Pacilus explained, they disdained and hated all gods other than their own, to the point of despising their images, even in art. The tribune thought that we should consider questioning Rufus on this further or making inquiry in the neighborhood, to make sure nothing improper was afoot.

This argument did not persuade me. The behavior of our host at the execution was explained easily enough by the peaceful conditions of life this far from the frontier; a country squire who stayed away from the games at Lugdunum might be expected to blanch at the sight of so many condemned men receiving their punishment. And the Christians were said to be fanatics, who engaged in many strange practices; a fanatic would tear up a mosaic, and not make a half-hearted effort at covering it over. Either way, as far as I was concerned, Pacilus was devoting too much thought to a matter of no import. If some backwoods land-owner wanted to dabble in loathsome Eastern mysteries, as long as he was discreet enough to keep it secret it was all the same to me.[1]

The forest drew close to the road as we left the cleared ground of the estate behind. Wood sounds surrounded us, and just outside the bobbing circle of torchlight there was a rustling as of deer through the undergrowth. The figures of fellow travelers on the road became dimly visible, as shapes in the blackness ahead. I called out to them, and they did not reply – but neither did they turn or leave the road, as bandits might have done.

---

[1] The fact that as of the date of these events these two officers are apparently unaware of any Imperial decree granting toleration to Christians casts doubt on the story of the "Thundering Legion" as recounted by Tertullian, Eusebius et al. The thunderstorm episode itself is so well attested as to be effectively beyond dispute, but the claimed involvement of Christians, and the subsequent order by Marcus Aurelius in 174 CE, is revealed by this exchange to be likely to be an apocryphal later legend layered onto the original tale.

We halted for a few moments, to see if they would hail us as they came closer. They did not. A shift in the wind carried to us a weak and thin sound of voices in distress – the sort of low, moaning hum mixed with unintelligible and garbled whispery cries that can come off a fresh battlefield at night.

We drew together, and stood to support the farm-boy, who had taken fright at the sounds and quailed and shook. Radamyntos handed me the reins of his mount, and took one of the torches from the sputtering boy. He strode forward several paces and repeated my road-greeting, insistently and in a great voice. Again there was no reply. Our horses grew nervous and stamped in place; my mount pulled hard at its bridle, and I only held on to the lead with effort.

The figures closed upon us, and in a few more moments came near enough to become just barely visible in the torchlight. At first I took them for lunatics: three men, dressed in torn and filthy tunics, smeared with mud and blood and feces, stumbled on the road. They were more disheveled than any decent beggar, with clods of dirt stuck to their skin and hair. Their jaws worked spastically and groans no more sensible than those of wild beasts came from their mouths.

"To the *crepido*,[1] beggars!" I bellowed, annoyed at being startled at night by such scum.

Then I noticed that one of them had an arm severed below the elbow, with flesh and skin dangling loosely from the cut.

"You!" Radamyntos cried in recognition at the largest of the figures.

What he meant by this I did not get to ask, because at that moment we were taken in flank. The rustling among the trees had not been deer after all, but more of these madmen. While we had concentrated our attention on the road, they had crept out of the forest and come up on our right, and slightly behind. There were three of them, possibly even filthier than the ones on the road. Two bore obvious wounds: one had a sword-cut to the face, from which half of his cheek hung down as if on a hinge, and one looked to have taken a *contus* in the chest, which had torn away both the lower half of his tunic and part of his ribcage. These great wounds did not prevent them from falling upon the farm-boy, who dropped his torch and screamed. The third madman, less obviously wounded than the others, grappled with Pacilus before he could come to the boy's aid.

Radamyntos dropped his torch as well, and let out the war cry of his tribe. With both

---

[1] Road-rim. Castus is ordering the road cleared so that he and his men may pass.

torches rolling on the crown-stones of the road, but neither yet extinguished, the light was much diminished but we could still see. Shadows danced and spun on the road as the madmen in front came forward.

Crazed now by the horrible groans and cries, the horses finally became uncontrollable and fled. Beasts reliable even on the battlefield could not stand before the strangeness on that road. I did not dwell on the loss of the horses long; I could not have kept hold of the bridle and handled my weapon in any event.

I drew my *pugio*[1] and rolled it in my right hand. The sword of Radamyntos – a cavalryman's broadsword, double-edged and with a diamond-section blade – swept into the air, as the decurion prepared the sort of slashing attack he might have employed while mounted. The one-armed madman reached us first, and Radamyntos slashed downward, and the great sword cut through his enemy's collarbone and exited down near the lungs. This was a killing stroke; if not instantly fatal, the recipient of it should at least have fallen to the ground in shock – but still the madman came on, grasping at Radamyntos' mailed arm and snarling over his gauntlet.

To our right the screams of the farm-boy rose in pitch with his terror. Out of the corner

---

[1] A Roman military dagger.

of my eye I could see that the madmen had dragged him to the ground, and were *biting* at his face and neck, as though they were wolves or lions and not men at all. The last of them had fixed his jaws on the arm of Pacilus. The tribune had his *gladius*[1] out, and stabbed his opponent in the belly with it again and again, trying to free himself; to little effect.

If men armed with swords could not lay these monsters[2] low, I doubted I could do much good with my dagger. I gave the one nearest to me a good shove instead, pushing it backwards as it reached out to pin down an arm of Radamyntos. The cavalryman shook free of his opponent, and lifting his sword high again this time struck for the neck. The blow did not quite decapitate, but came near enough to finally stop the monster's advance.

"Come on then!" Radamyntos shouted at the large one he had earlier seemed to recognize. The recognition was not returned. The monster hissed and moaned and continued its attack, but its eyes showed no awareness. Radamyntos cleaved its skull in two from right

---

[1] The Roman infantry short sword. Castus is very precise in this section with regard to the use of the weapons his party carried; Radamyntos and Pacilus approach the engagement differently because they are equipped differently.

[2] Castus abruptly begins to use the Latin *monstrum* here, no doubt having concluded that he is dealing with something more than mere madmen.

to left. This was as effective as a stopping blow as the neck-strike had been. The momentum of the sword-cut carried him forward just enough to cause him to stumble, though, and the last of the monsters to our front clambered on to his back. I brought the pommel of my *pugio*, which ended in a thick ring, down upon the back of its head with all my weight, and shattered its skull with a loud and painful *crack*.

Pacilus had seen enough of what Radamyntos had done to change his tactics as a result, and brought down the beast that had seized him with a series of hacks to the throat that finally severed its spine.

Even though all their fellows had been dispatched, the remaining monsters continued to rend the poor farm-boy's flesh. Had we been prepared to leave them to it, they would have taken no notice of us at all. The three of us freed the boy with a flurry of angry cuts, but it was too late; the life had gone out of him, there on the road, and his face and neck now resembled a gnawed carcass from a carrion field.

The quiet of the night came back like a cold wind. Pacilus shook his head to clear it, and gestured about us while he declaimed: "He grows a wolf; his hoariness remains – and the same rage in other members reigns."[1]

With this Pacilus was revealed to be a man who could quote poetry moments after facing such terrors as we had just seen. I did not know whether to be impressed, or appalled. I had not known he had it in him, and would have leaned on him more and reached out to him in greater friendship these last months had I known. His quip brought a laugh to my lips; from I know not what reserves of dark amusement.

"Did you know these madmen?" I asked Radamyntos, remembering how he had spoken to the one.

"Aye," he answered, and pointed. "The fat one...I killed him yesterday." He stopped to remove first his helmet, and then one gauntlet, and wiped the sweat from his face with his bared hand. "As we rode up to the villa, he was one of those who stood to face us, to buy time as their friends tried to fly to the wood. I cut him down as he tried to pull me from the saddle."

Radamyntos had good camp-Latin, but still spoke like a barbarian at times. Perhaps he had mistaken what he meant to say. "Surely you did not kill him?" I asked, although I could

---

[1] Ovid, *Metamorphoses*. As punishment for the impiety of offering Jupiter human flesh at a banquet, the tyrant Lycaon is transformed into a werewolf.

feel the answer like an icy stone in the pit of my gut. "For here he is."

"No." He was calmly certain. "When I kill a man, I remember him. Believe me."

"I believe you," Pacilus interjected.

"I killed him, and I saw him on the field when his gear was stripped, and I saw him again when the prisoners threw his body with the others in the trash-pit." He shrugged. "He decided he wanted to die again. It is no matter. Let him come a third time, it will be the same."

I gathered up the torches, which remarkably had stayed lit throughout. "We should see to the horses."

Radamyntos shook his head. "Not easy, in this dark."

"We won't have time," Pacilus said, wincing. "Listen. Between the gusts."

I held my head up into the wind and closed my eyes. Just at the edge of hearing, the low, moaning hum of voices was still there – but somehow layered, as if there were many more of the creatures, scattered at varying distances.

"Forget the horses," I said, though it stuck in my throat to say it. "We have to go back to the villa. It's the only way."

"What about the boy?" Radamyntos asked.

"Leave him." I was blunt about it. "There's no time. And he can't be helped now."

Pacilus was aghast. “They...gnawed upon him.” He winced again, both from disgust and from the bite wound in his arm. “We can’t leave him in the open.” Radamyntos nodded to reinforce the tribune’s point; he was equally hesitant to leave.

I was not about to risk a tribune and a decurion to salvage the corpse of a farm slave, and I told them so in no uncertain terms. Despite having the right of it, I had to be quite severe. They both grumbled, but finally each took a torch from me and we reluctantly started to retrace our way. Angry, horror-struck, reason nearly overthrown by prodigy and omen, we staggered back down the road in the dark.

FOUR

I made a vow to Diana Trivia[1] when we came again to the track that led from the road to the villa. Often enough I had doubted the use of such vows in the past, but in that cold-bitten dark I thought no appeal for aid to be not worth the attempt.

As we found our way back over our steps the cries in the distance waxed and waned in number, and were now closer, now farther. Every spot of ground where two black and bare trees came together to our eyes loomed in the dark as a potential site for an ambuscade. The ditches and hedges marking off the fields made a veritable *clades Variana*.[2] The cries of the

---

[1] The Roman equivalent of Hecate, the goddess of the three-way crossroad, as well as an important goddess of the underworld. A "vow" in this context would involve promising a future service or sacrifice to a deity in return for immediate divine assistance.

[2] The Roman name for the battle of the Teutoburg Forest, where the legions under Publius Quinctilius Varus were

sows from the large pigsty maintained by Rufus disturbed us so much that we dithered long before it and had to force ourselves to walk on.

When we reached the villa at last, I surveyed the building with an eye for its defensive value. It was good, solid stone and mortar, and not just pounded and plastered earth and timber like many houses in the north. Several of the windows were covered by iron grilles, but some of them had only jointed wooden shutters.

We pounded on the door for some time before the servants appeared, followed by a mystified master of the house. The commotion created by our return was such that I had to shout for silence to still it. We pushed our way into the corridor and barred the door behind us.

"We were waylaid on the road," I said, not immediately knowing what else I should or could say, or how to explain what we had lately seen.

"Where is Florus?" our host asked.

"Dead," I replied. I had not known his name.

"Was it the rebels?" Rufus choked. It was clear that he had felt affection for this servant and met our news with grief. Even by

---

ambushed and destroyed by German tribesmen led by Arminius.

the flickering light of a single wick,[1] I could read the anguish in his face.

Pacilus laughed bitterly at this question. "You might say that," he replied.

I glared at him.

"We don't know who or what we met on the road," I declared firmly. Now that we had the security of walls about us, I regretted my earlier fear. I did not want to make any demonstration of panic that could be used to reproach us later.

Pacilus and Radamyntos would have none of it.

"Aye, it was the rebels," Radamyntos puffed. "Their corpses,[2] anyway. Stalking the road and the wood in the night."

"*Miastores*,"[3] Pacilus interceded emphatically. He was not going to be cautious in his

---

[1] Roman lamps were small terra cotta bowls filled with olive oil and from one to ten wicks. The more wicks that were employed, the more light the lamp would cast, and the more rapidly the oil would be consumed. Castus may be offering this statement to accentuate the darkness of the house and as further evidence of Rufus' miserliness.

[2] He employs the Latin *corpora*, leaving no doubt that he believed he was dealing with the dead.

[3] Pacilus here employs a Greek word, rather than a Latin one. A member of his class would be expected to be passably fluent in Greek, and it is not surprising that he has recourse to it when Latin fails to provide him with the appropriate word. *Miastores* were sometimes spirits who secured vengeance on behalf of the dead, but the word could also

claims, either. "Wreaking their vengeance. Like Medea's children."[1]

With this the household was swept into commotion once again. The wife of Rufus, a thin and desiccated woman who had kept herself hidden until now,[2] appeared and began to howl angrily at her husband and remonstrate with him about the fate of the boy Florus. The servants rushed to and fro in a frenzy. I had to shout for silence once more.

"I do not know..." I averred, "...if we were the victim of some trick or foul stratagem to play off the terror of the night, or whether the *lemures*[3] have learned how to seize the bodies of the slain to use as murderous

---

refer to the dead themselves, wandering the Earth seeking revenge as revenants.

[1] Euripides has Jason tell Medea that their dead children will hound her as *miastores*.

[2] In most conservative Roman households women would not appear at dinner if guests were present. Upper-class women eluded this custom only in Rome itself and some of the other large urban centers.

[3] Latin has no word for "revenant". *Lemures*, like *manes* or *larvae*, refers to the disembodied spirits of the dead. Castus is verbally improvising here. He continues with *lemures*, despite the fact that Pacilus has offered a more appropriate Greek term; no doubt this reflects a preference for Latin usages, even in novel situations where Latin lacks appropriate vocabulary.

puppets.[1] All I know is that, whoever or whatever our enemies on the road may have been, we need to be ready to face them *here*. And soon."

"No foul creature of the night will dare to enter this house," Rufus swore. "Would that Florus had not left it. Would that I had not *sent* him from it."

"You confidence is welcome," I replied. "More welcome still would be more lamps. Can we set the servants to it?"

Radamyntos stalked down the hallway. "I will see to the *posticum*."[2]

Pacilus began a survey of the rooms, concerned about the windows. In this he repeated my own thoughts. In any town a sensible house would have presented nothing but a blank stone face to the street, but we were not so fortunate here. Country ways and the needs of country households were different.

I questioned Rufus about the assets of the estate. "We were not challenged by any dog on either occasion when we approached your door. Do you not keep any?"

"I keep two white Molossians,[1] but they are with my shepherds in their hut, in the

---

[1] It has been suggested that the translation "doll" is more correct here, but Castus uses the expression *mobile lignum*, which Horace employs to describe a type of marionette.
[2] Back door or servant's door.

autumn pasture; and that is a mile and more from here."

This displeased me. Dogs would have provided ample warning of any *lemures* or men that approached us. It helped us not at all for the shepherds to have a warning. I sighed, and considered the next possibility. "This may alarm you, but we will need to arm your slaves."

Rufus accepted this news with equanimity. He spread his hands wide and shrugged. "Arm them however you like, but no slave of this house will draw the blood of any man."

"That's quite all right," Pacilus said to him, returning with some of those slaves at his back. "Since we face *prostropaioi*,[2] and not men." He turned to me. "The windows are reasonably secure. Only three of them have *junctae*[3] rather than grills, and we have wedged those shut with kindling from the hearth."

"How many male slaves are there?" I asked.

---

[1] A primitive mastiff, used as both a watchdog and a sheepdog, mentioned by Strabo, Oppian, and Petronius, among others.

[2] Another Greek word for the restless or vengeful spirits of the dead, in this instance the particular servants of the goddess Hecate.

[3] Some Roman shutters were in a single piece that slid in a framework on the outer wall. Shutters as we would recognize them, in two pieces that moved in opposite directions, were called "junctae" or "joined".

"The three here in the house, and four more who sleep in the sheds," Rufus replied. "And my wife has a girl in the kitchen."

Radamyntos came up, looking gruffly satisfied. "The *posticum* is well-barred, and as strong as you could want."

"Good." I acknowledged his report. "Take these slaves here, and send them out to summon their fellows inside from the out-buildings and to gather those farm implements that might be useful as weapons," I told him. "*Do not go out of the house yourself.* Watch them from the doorway and bar the door when they return." He left again to do as I had instructed.

I turned back to Rufus. "I did not see any arms displayed as we dined.[1] Are there any in the house?"

This question made him uncomfortable, and he squirmed and grimaced as he answered it. "My father kept a set of arms. They are in the *arca*."[2]

I had him lead me to the *tablinum*[3] so he could show them to me. There was a sword, but I groaned to see that it was in a sheath.

---

[1] In some upper-class Roman households, in an affectation that dated back to Republican times, arms were hung on the wall in the dining room or near the hearth - as if the owner of the house was ready to join the legions at a moment's notice.

[2] A strongbox commonly kept in Roman households to store valuables.

[3] A study or den for the master of the house.

"No, no," Rufus exclaimed at my reaction. "I am not such a fool as to let my father's sword rust.[1] It has been regularly waxed, despite my lack of a use for it." There was also a shirt of *lorica squamata*,[2] which looked large enough for me, but no shield.

"Sir," I said to Rufus with as much courtesy as I could manage, "...if I am to defend you in this house I have to beg you for the use of these heirlooms."

He assented to this. I knelt in the corridor and Pacilus and the last remaining slave assisted me in bringing the shirt over my head.[3] Even though the *lemures* had not come upon us armed, it was reassuring to have the weight of armor across my shoulders.

Radamyntos presently returned once more, trailed by a column of irregularly armed slaves.

---

[1] A Roman sword stored in a sheath will accumulate moisture along the thickest part of the blade and rust very quickly.

[2] Armor made by wiring small scales onto a fabric or leather jerkin. This variety of armor was not very common, compared to the more standard chain mail or segmented armor typically associated with the popular image of a Roman legionary.

[3] This is the only first-person description of how *lorica squamata* was donned that we have, and was eagerly and gratefully received by students of the military equipment of this era.

"It will have to do," he said, a bit contemptuously, nodding at those who trailed him. Three of them carried the *falx*,[1] and they were the luckiest of the lot. One had an axe of the Belgae,[2] and another a mattock; the remainder carried wooden clubs. "Company's coming."

"What did you see?"

"See? Nothing but the black, and you can barely see that. But the animals are mad with fear, and even above their lowing you can hear the cries of the dead in the air."

The kitchen girl had brought forth a large bowl of *posca*[3]. Radamyntos took a goblet from her and swept out a large draught. "*Salve,*[4] *dux*," he toasted with cold irony.

"We'll see about that," Pacilus joked, wanly. The strain of the night's events plainly wore upon him, despite his wry and witty manner. A severe pallor had crept across his face and his wound, though minor, appeared to pain him.

"We will indeed." I strode to the barred door and shook it, testing the bolts. "Then again,

---

[1] A pruning hook or small scythe.

[2] The tool we would consider a traditional axe – a heavy chopping blade head with an eye through which a wooden handle passes – was imported into the Roman world from the Gallic tribe of the Belgae.

[3] A largely non-alcoholic mixture of water and sour wine or near-vinegar.

[4] A toast to the health of the listener.

perhaps our adversaries will choose to haunt the night clear through, and not seek to trouble us."

My fellows shrugged. I held out no great hope that we would be left alone, either.

Standing by the door, I saw what was spelled out by the wall mosaic there and I laughed darkly:

Nihil intret mali.[1]

I slapped the letters of the motto lightly with my fingertips. "We'll soon see if Janus[2] smiles upon this house," I said, and there was little else to say.

---

[1] "May no evil enter here."

[2] The Roman god of the doorway, to whom the door-motto was usually directed.

FIVE

I have stood many watches on ill-omened nights without fear, and have waited calmly in the dark before a battle many times as well. I have listened to the waters of the Danuvius[1] running unseen over the stones on the riverside under a cloud-filled and starless sky, while great tribes milled on the opposite bank. I have peered over the wall[2] that forms our northern border and barrier and strained to hear distant hoof-beats through the thick night-mist. But never has any watch made my heart tremble as did the one we stood that night in the villa of Rufus.

With my face pressed to the window grille in one of the *cubicula*,[3] I listened to the cries of the *lemures* in the distance. They first seemed to come closer, and then draw away, before coming closer once more; almost as though

1 The Danube River.

2 Hadrian's Wall.

3 A *cubiculum* was a sleeping area or bedroom.

they did not move across the land with any purpose, but simply wandered. At times their cries became almost intelligible, and I strained to pick out words; but whether these words were the horrible curses leveled by the dead upon the world, or the exclamations of other travelers upon the road as they were waylaid as we had been, I could not say.

Rufus and Pacilus stayed with me in a room facing north towards the road, while Radamyntos kept his own watch from a room with a window on the south wall. The slaves waited in two groups by the doors; those entrances were barred well enough that they could be trusted with their defense. Pacilus reviewed the sequence of the road attack with me again as we waited, and speculated at some length on the nature of our attackers.

He saw little doubt that, by some magic or by the intervention of some god, the old man's curse had been effectuated and the rebels we had slain had risen to slay us in turn. The testimony of Radamyntos sufficed, in his view, to establish this. Had this not been enough, the terrible wounds their bodies had been able to endure and ignore served to prove that we were not facing living men. They could walk and grasp and bite without blood or breath, supported only by the curse or the god; though why the spell should be made to fail by a cut or blow to the head or neck, he could not say.

As he spoke and as we waited, Pacilus slowly looked more and more ill. His pallor grew, and he started to shiver slightly, as if a fever was growing in his flesh. I thought then that perhaps his wound was more severe than we had at first known, or that as sometimes happens the cooling of his blood in the interval since the fight on the road had brought the full effect of the wound out. I encouraged him to try to rest.

Rufus, for his part, disdained Pacilus' explanation of events, but he scowled when I questioned him and declined to offer any explanation of his own. Although he had been able to translate the curse of the old man – the druid? – for us, he denied having any additional knowledge of the local cult to impart. I did not believe that he shared all his thoughts with us, but I chose not to press him.

"Oh ho!" Radamyntos called out in a low voice, across the corridor. "Who comes calling?"

"Stay here," I directed Pacilus. "Be alert." I hurried through the house to guard-spot of Radamyntos, bringing Rufus with me. As I crossed the corridor in haste, the slaves cried out in fear.

"What do you see?" I asked, as I joined Radamyntos in the south window. Rufus, coming up behind, peered through the window between us as best he could.

"Walking in the kitchen garden," he hissed. "One of our handsome friends."

One of the filthy corpse-puppets stiffly made its way through the scraggly herbs and dead plants. This one was totally without clothes, and lacked even the torn and bloody tunic the others had possessed. It had a broad cut across its belly, and trailed strings of its entrails behind it; I wondered how it could cross a field or a wood in such a state. It stumbled awkwardly towards the farm-house.

Rufus gasped; his mouth worked, but such was his surprise that he could not speak.

"You had not believed us, then?" I asked him. He nodded. I couldn't blame him; not fairly. I would have doubted such a tale from anyone else.

"*Shada*!"[1] he finally managed to fiercely whisper. "A *shada* has come to test us!"

"What?" I asked him, but got no reply. He dashed out of the room, and called his wife forth from the hiding-place she had sought out in the kitchen. "Shada!" he repeated, over and over, although what this barbaric term might signify he did not indicate. His wife began to keen with fear.

He dragged her by the arm into the corridor and pushed her bodily down on to her knees on the floor, and then bent down

[1] The Aramaic word for "demon".

himself. The nearby slaves at that end of the house hastened to kneel as well in imitation of their example. Once so positioned on the floor, they began to loudly and fervently implore Christus to come to their aid. This certainly settled the evening's earlier argument in the favor of Pacilus. It also demonstrated just how much fear was in the air; our hosts were so desperate for the intercession of their god that they were willing to allow their membership in the foul cult to be exposed to me.[1]

Radamyntos called me back. "Two more," he said. "Beyond the garden, on the edge of the fields." I could only see one, but the decurion's eyes were sharper than mine. "They hear the matron squealing, I think," he went on. "They are coming to the house with a purpose, now."

Indeed, the monsters I could see, while they did not seem any more sensible, did appear to be drawn in a straight path towards

---

[1] It had long been regarded as a settled issue among scholars that all of the gospels were originally written in Greek, and that the Pontifical Biblical Commission's claim that the gospel of Matthew was originally written in Aramaic had no factual or historical basis. The episode recounted in this section, however, breathed new life into the "Aramaic proto-Matthew" position: the fact that a Gallo-Roman and likely native Latin speaker would immediately employ the Aramaic word for "demon" in this situation makes it likely that he had previously read some sort of religious document written in that tongue.

the noise that passed from the corridor and out the window. "Hag," I muttered.

Radamyntos moved to the door. "Keep silent!" he hissed – to only slight effect.

Pacilus darted into the corridor as well, his face as white as chalk in the half-light of the lamps. "Another comes from the north," he informed me. "Should we sortie, and strike them down before they can gather?"

"That has never been my intention," I replied. "Not with our position here so well secured. We will wait until dawn. I want to see if these curse-driven ones are as terrible in the sunlight as they are now." Pacilus doubted this course, and his face fell as he shuffled back to his post at the window.

We did not have to wait long to see how well the house defenses would withstand the creatures. The three that crossed the garden bunched up by the window from which we had regarded them. They clawed helplessly at the grille that barred it, and scraped their nails across the iron. There was no chance of their making it inside that way; they may as well have been small birds clutching at the grille-work with weak and insignificant talons. The one that approached from the north did no better at the window guarded by Pacilus. None of them had tried forcing any of the shuttered windows yet; they may have lacked the wit needed to distinguish a shutter from the wall.

We called to the creatures through the grilles and tried, and failed, to engage them in speech. They would answer no question, and were insensitive to any insult or command. We ended by spitting at them, and splashing them with the contents of a chamber pot; they ignored that as well.

I was able to examine these monsters more closely, now that they were held before us at the windows. Although they could obviously see – for how else could they know how to pry at the window covering? – their eyes were utterly blank, without even the discernment of a cow or rabbit within them. The odor that rose from them was even greater than what I would have expected from a day-old corpse. It was as if the curse that brought them to us had filled them with some powerful corruption, or as if the *lemures* had brought back with them from the underworld some part of the foul airs that dominate deep below the earth.

"You see?" I chided Pacilus, when I had a moment to check up on his position. A second creature had joined the first one at his window, but they were just as helpless to enter as the others. "There is no need to sortie. These scum have no arms or implements and no mind to wield them."

"You were right," he said, smiling wanly. "They may have crossed the Styx, but a bolted door is too much for them, it seems."

His fever and weakness had continued to get worse, and his eyelids fluttered with exhaustion as we spoke. I posted a slave with him to keep up the watch on that window, and ordered him to try to sleep. There was no need for him to fight to stay awake to guard a barrier that our foes had no way to cross.

After settling Pacilus I inspected the two doors again. There was rattling at each of them; additional *lemures* had no doubt staggered up to the house from angles that could not be seen from any of the guarded windows. Rufus and his wife and the slaves with them had redoubled their pleas to Christus, as if to drown out the unnerving sound of the rattling bolts thereby. Rufus interspersed his vows with threats and imprecations against the creatures, shifting back and forth between decent speech and some barbaric Eastern tongue. “They will not enter this house!” he again declared to me, when he saw me draw close.

“Not if the locks here hold, which looks certain,” I replied – but I had misunderstood him.

“It is not a matter of locks and bolts,” he said, shaking his head. “They have no power that any in my household need fear!” he averred.

I took this to mean that he was confident that his god would protect them. I myself put more confidence in the stone of the walls and the thick wood of the doors. Then again, after seeing the efficaciousness of the old man's curse and considering our current predicament, I had to allow that perhaps Rufus was in the right. If a god could raise such terrors against us, another god could certainly strike them down again.

The slaves posted at the opposite door had not offered to join their master and mistress in their kneeling and clothes-rending and invocations of the god, and Rufus had not dared to test me by summoning them away from where I had posted them. I spoke briefly to one of them, a great yellow German, as I satisfied myself that his door was secure. It is always impolitic to ply the slave of another man with questions designed to probe for secrets of the house, but I could not resist asking the German if he too expected Christus to protect him. Try as he might, he could not conceal his expression of doubt and equivocation. It was clear he did not share his master's certainty about the prospects for divine intervention.

"The *domina*[1] has us pray[2] to the Father,[1] and that is only right," he said, diplomatically. "But if I had any beans, I would offer them."[2]

---

[1] The mistress of the house; the wife of Rufus.

[2] Although elsewhere I translate *voveo* as "to vow", from the mouth of a Christian the word has the sense of "to pray".

For my part, if I could have laid my hands on any beans, I would have done the same.

Having satisfied myself that all was in order and that our defenses were proof against the *lemures* as long as they kept hold of their puppets, I returned to the watch-post of Radamyntos. He had moved away from the window, to avoid the foul odor and grasping fingers there, and knelt on one knee on a pallet he had moved into place to help support him.[3] It was hard to be sure without drawing closer to the window than was wise, but the number

---

[1] Glancy, in *Slavery in Early Christianity,* argues that the "household conversion" episodes in the Acts of the Apostles imply that the evangelists were quite happy to baptize slaves who had been ordered to convert by their masters, and that the quality of those conversions was often in doubt. This incident supports both of those speculations.

[2] This exchange is somewhat obscure. Although Castus identifies the slave as a German, the man appears to be proclaiming that he would prefer to propitiate the dead using the traditional Latin folk offering of black beans. This may mean that he had become a slave at a very young age and had grown up in a household that subscribed to Latin folkways, and he therefore retained no memory of German traditions. To this slave, the choice is not between Christian prayer and German customs, but between Christian prayer and Latin customs.

[3] In full armor Radamyntos would have had considerable weight to support.

of creatures that struggled there appeared to have grown to four or five.

"It's all well?" he asked.

"Yes," I confirmed. "As fine as we can expect."

"Except the noise." He shook his head and gestured towards the wailers in the corridor. "I'd rather listen to the singing from outside than Rufus and his shrieking. Should we shut them up?" He drew one finger across his throat.

"Leave the civilians alone," I scolded. I then lectured him for a while on the courtesy due to country gentry who had done us no harm and committed no political offense, and urged him not to treat loyal citizens as he would the targets of a punitive expedition over the line. When I was satisfied that he had heard enough, I arranged myself as well as I could on the pallet to join in the watch, and grit my teeth to wait for the dawn.

SIX

Screams – terrible, strangled screams – caught me with my eyelids hanging heavy, some time later. No finger of dawn yet extended over the horizon. We were not to be allowed to wait the night out after all.

I was startled and confused, but I sprang to my feet. "Is that inside or outside?" I called to Radamyntos.

He was already moving through the doorway. "Inside!" he called back.

I stumbled into the corridor, just behind him. My steps were halted by what I saw there; a black, cold stone in my belly held me rooted to one spot. The screams came from a slave – the slave I had left with Pacilus. The slave was dragging himself down the corridor with Pacilus clinging to his back. Pacilus was biting and gouging at the side of the slave's neck. There was much blood, and the veins and tendons of the slave's throat were exposed to the air, where they were not caught up in his attacker's clutching fingers.

"Tribune!" I tried to bellow in a tone of command, but all that I could muster was a high-pitched squawk. "Stop this madness!" I cried, although I already knew he could not hear me.

Radamyntos hesitated in confusion. It is likely he was unwilling to strike an officer without my direct order to do so. The cold stone in my belly broke apart a bit, and I strode past the decurion with bile on my lips and the sword of the house of Rufus in my hand.

I struck at Pacilus' right forearm. The stroke did not sever, but I heard the bones crack, and the slave was able to struggle free. He rolled clear on the floor, still screaming, and ineffectively trying to use his fingers to hold back the rush of blood from the wound at his neck. Pacilus turned to face me, instead. There was no light in his eyes, and he had not the mind left to either know me or care. With a rolling and gasping growl, he reached for me with his remaining useful arm.

Radamyntos, encouraged by my own attack, stepped forward and pushed the corpse of Pacilus back, to create some dead space between it and ourselves; he used that opening to make a striding strike at the tribune's neck. The head and body fell separately to the floor.

The other slaves came running. None of them were quicker than the kitchen girl, who squealed in dismay at the sight of the headless body and the great wound of the member of her household. She would have sought to attend to the wounded one, but I held her back with one arm.

"Leave him!" I ordered. "Do not touch him."

Rufus and his wife, coming up behind, heard this and hissed at me.

"That is my man, *Dux*," Rufus growled, in a tone far more dangerous than one who has given up his only sword should have contemplated using. "If we do not aid him, he will surely die."

"Wait!" I shouted. And then, more softly: "A moment."

I struggled to think, as the wounded slave continued to whimper and his masters fretted, and the smell of blood rose in the air. I did not understand how the curse could have raised Pacilus against us. Had some miasma[1] from

---

[1] Miasma is a Greek term with a double meaning: it can refer to the air that rises from swamps, which the ancient Greeks and Romans both associated with disease; it can also refer to a religious pollution, arising from a foul or unclean deed that can stain an individual and mark him for punishment by the Fates. It cannot be determined from the context in which sense Castus meant to use the term, because either meaning is possible here.

the foul creatures around us seized the tribune, and subjected him to the curse? Or had his wound, slight as it had looked, weakened and killed him, and allowed the *lemures* to seize his corpse and use it against us, as they had seized the others? I had conceded that the spirits called by the old man had raised his dead fellow-rebels to wage war on us again, but I had not guessed that they could draft into their legion any man who fell before them. The implications of that were not pleasant. If this curse could spread like dysentery at a barbarian war-camp, it could sweep the countryside.

And then there was the wounded slave, whose blood still ran away and whose death came closer with every moment while I mused like Varro.[1]

---

[1] Castus' reference to Varro is both ambiguous and exciting. Marcus Terentius Varro in *Rerum Rusticarum* advised his readers to avoid swamps because they "breed certain minute creatures which cannot be seen by the eyes, but which float in the air and enter the body through the mouth and nose and cause serious diseases." This uncanny anticipation of germ theory was always assumed to have been a scientific dead end, driven from the stage by Galen's popularization of the theory of the humours and forgotten by history until resurrected by Fracastoro and van Leeuwenhoek. But the fact that the fate of Pacilus makes Castus think of Varro may indicate that a germ theory of disease made it further into the popular mind of the antiquity than we have previously believed. Combined with the tantalizing – but again, ambiguous – previous reference to *miasma*, Castus here

I made my decision.

"Radamyntos," I said calmly, and pointed to the slave. "Take his head."

The decurion stepped forward, without the slightest question; I do not know if this was mere discipline, or whether he had been able to roughly reason his way to the same conclusion as I. The slave, not yet too weak to struggle to keep his life, groveled and rolled on the floor, begging me for mercy and his master for aid.

"No, no!" Rufus shouted. The other slaves scattered down the corridor. The wife of Rufus, showing more bravery than sense, moved towards the slave, as if to succor or protect him. I stood in her way and raised my own sword, very slightly, but enough for notice and for the greatest possible offense.[1]

The slave, pathetically, attempted to use his hands to shield himself. The blow, when it came, rained fingers onto the floor before slicing through the fellow's jaw and snapping his spine.

---

comes painfully close to enunciating a nearly modern theory of disease contagion. He does not quite make it to modernity, however, and ultimately it is plain that he continues to regard the strange events he describes here as supernatural and not epidemiological.

[1] Despite the extremely bizarre and dangerous series of events, Castus here shows concern that by making this threat to the mistress of the house he has failed in his duty as a guest.

"No!" Rufus shouted again. "Murderers! A despicable tyrant and his barbarian lackey! Woe to my house!"

The eyes of Radamyntos asked if I wanted to silence our host and be free of his insults. I gestured to him to remain still.

"Calm yourself, sir," I instructed Rufus. "Think! Are you blind? Have you seen nothing here?" I pointed to the headless body of Pacilus. "It should be clear now that the curse that has brought the dead upon us can use any of the dead to its purposes. Once the blood of your man had run away into the tiles, he would have joined their number and turned upon us. I did only what was necessary."

The anger of Rufus was not soothed, and he regarded me with complete disdain. "Necessary? It was assuredly *not* necessary." He knelt on the floor and took the bloody hand of the dead slave in his own. "The slaves of this house have shared the blood of the Christ. No curse out of the forgotten years of Gaul could give them over to be the tool of the *shada* that took your friend. Any *daimon*[1] that tried, we would cast out."

I shook my head. Radamyntos sneered bitterly, and I knew he could read my thoughts.

---

[1] Rufus abruptly switches to the Greek word here, no doubt correctly guessing that the Aramaic term is meaningless to Castus.

The dead walked, and this fool wanted to face them with nothing more than Jewish sorcery.

"Your god has not come yet," Radamyntos scoffed. "And you have called him enough, and more than enough. He certainly did not thunder down from the skies with a flaming sword to aid the dead one, here."

Rufus raised his fists, and for a moment it seemed – incredibly – that he would strike at us, bare hands against swords. His wife calmed him. She held his shoulder, and drew him off, whispering into his ear.

This left us alone with the shattered bodies of the tribune and the slave. I shuddered for Pacilus, and the dark and ill-omened end to which he had come. The *lemures* had seized him here, far from his home, where no honest legionary pyre or any servant of Venus Libitina[1] Libitina[1] could ease his way into the next world. There seemed to be no point to hoping for a good fate for him in the next world now; the dark *lemures* of the druid had been there to catch his last breath, and no son or brother.[2]

---

[1] The slaves who attended to funeral rites were associated with the temple of this aspect of the goddess Venus.

[2] When a Roman died among his family, it was the responsibility of those present to have one of their number attempt to catch the dying man's last breath in their mouth.

"Our host bears watching," Radamyntos said, and brought me out of my thoughts. "He doesn't know who to hate more, now – the dead, or us."

"Let him rail against us all he wants," I replied, dismissively. "As he thinks it through, he'll realize we were right."

I rallied the scattered slaves from their hiding places in the various rooms and to their guard-posts once again. Rufus avoided me, hustling into the kitchen with his wife and her girl. In his absence I made it clear to the slaves that I expected them to refrain from further pointless wailing and oath-taking, and to stand fast before the doors. I sought out the German, who I judged to be less of a fool than the others.

"Your master is not well," I told him. "At some point I may call upon you to restrain him, for his own good. Be assured that no punishment will come upon you if you do so. I will make sure of that, even if I must appeal to the governor himself."

The slave looked doubtful, and I could not blame him. Assuming we survived this night, I would leave with the army, which moved quickly through the lives of simple folk like a passing thunderstorm, full of noise and light but gone by evening. His master, on the other hand, would always be there. Knowing this as he must, he might not be of much use, in the event.

As it developed, we did not have to wait long to find out.

Waving her arms over her head and shouting in distress, the slave girl burst out of the kitchen and into the corridor. In her alarm she abandoned her humility and reserve and grabbed our arms and shook them wildly.

"Lords!" she gasped. "They...they would go out..."

She dragged us forward into the kitchen, and what we saw there could not be countenanced. The shutters were no longer wedged shut, but stood opened wide to the night. Several amphorae[1] had been dragged into the ash-trench[2] beneath the open shutters. We came through the door just in time to see the mistress of the house as she finished clambering up this improvised platform and squeezed out the open window. Rufus himself was nowhere to be seen, and had clearly gone out the window ahead of his wife.

---

[1] An *amphora* was a large ceramic urn with a thin neck that was used to store significant quantities of oil, wine, or grain.

[2] Roman ovens were fairly primitive. A fire would be built directly in the cooking area, and once the desired temperature had been reached the coals would be raked out into a trench in the floor. Food would be placed into the cleared space to cook in the residual heat.

"Fools," Radamyntos muttered disgustedly beside me.

As I moved to the window, I could see that they had stopped just a few yards outside the window, and stood looking about themselves uncertainly. It was as if they were not quite sure how to proceed. The dead, however, suffered no such confusion. They abandoned their feeble efforts at the grilled windows and staggered after our foolish hosts.

"Are you mad?" I called after them. There was still time for them to return to the safety of the house if they moved quickly. The kitchen girl and the German cried out pitifully to their masters as well, and pleaded with them to come back.

"Florus! Florus!" Rufus cried out to the many walking dead –

And at once I understood. Observing the fate of Pacilus, they reasoned that the slave Florus would have fallen under the power of the curse after being taken by the creatures on the road. They no doubt purposed to employ their sorcery, and counted on the intercession of their god to restore Florus to them. I was torn between horror at their folly, and a sudden wild hope that perhaps they would succeed in turning back our adversaries by their piety. But as that hope was no basis for inaction, I sheathed my sword and pulled myself into the empty window-space. “Follow me,” I urged my companions, as calmly as I could.

My head spun a little as I clambered to my feet in the yard outside the window. Denied as I now was of the protection of the closed space of the villa, I was dazzled by the open air, and by the stars ringing high above me. I stood exposed to the night.

There was a loud crash and the sound of shattering pottery. I stole a glance back at the window from which I had just come, and saw Radamyntos flailing about. Hampered by his long shirt of mail, he had fallen while attempting to come after me, and had knocked down the stacked amphorae. He swore with rage atop a pile of shards of terra cotta.

I turned back towards Rufus and his wife in some alarm. The *lemures* were nearly upon them – and nearly upon me as well – and I doubted if alone I could force them both back inside, even if I had recourse to threats. Before I could worry this question long, however, the German appeared beside me; he was unencumbered by arms other than the *falx*, and could easily manage the window that had for the moment defeated the decurion.

“We must get your masters inside before we are all lost,” I told him, and he nodded.

Three strides sufficed to place me next to the German’s mistress, and I seized her shoulders. Even given the madness of the moment, this impropriety shocked Rufus and staggered him; he left off his shouting and gesturing, and stared at me open-mouthed. His surprise grew even greater when the German grabbed him about the chest and lifted him bodily into the air. We brought them back to the window with some rough handling, and had nearly reached safety just as the nearest of the creatures drew close enough to be clearly seen.

With a loud squawk, my captive squirmed free of my grasp. The shoulder of her *stola*[1] tore under my fingers, and she broke away. "Florus!" she cried out once more, and I saw that the nearest of the creatures was none other than the slave-boy we had abandoned on the road. How she recognized him, I cannot say; the flesh of his face was torn and gnawed nearly down to the skull and jawbone, and the skin of his face that had not been eaten away hung down in tatters. She reached out to him with kind words, and with wasted and pathetic pleading, but the creature did not hesitate; it grappled with her, and bore her to the ground, and tore at her breast with its fleshless jaw and its blood-stained hands. None of this was hidden from Rufus, who bellowed like a dying bull as he struggled to escape the German and return to help his wife.

---

[1] A married Roman woman wore a second garment called a *stola* on top of the basic tunic.

Even though I knew I was already too late, I could not restrain the impulse to come to the aid of a matron placed at the mercy of such a horror. I drew my sword with one hand, and tried to pull the corpse of Florus away from its prey with the other.

It was foolish of me not to give her up and get back inside as quickly as I could, as was shown when another pair of the creatures reached the scene of our struggle. In what felt like a blink of the eye, they bore me down to the ground. I was sure I was lost. Through a spinning jumble of the limbs and the rasping faces of the dead, I saw Rufus, now free, run by me and throw himself upon the dead Florus, no longer calling out for his god but delivering a stream of curses and abuse instead. Then I saw the *falx* sweep by above my face, two, three, four times, and before the creatures could bite or claw at me they fell down all around like wheat cut down by a scythe.

The smiling face of the German appeared upside-down above me, looking amazed and proud at his own action. He had let Rufus go, it was plain, in order to be able to assist me. He helped me to my feet.

Rufus had not succeeded in freeing his wife, who was beyond help now in any event. The dead could not be separated from the living with anything other than a blade; the fists and feet of Rufus were not up to the task.

As he desperately pulled at the arms of the dead Florus, he too was set upon by more of the creatures.

The German gestured, as if to ask what we should do. I shook my head. We ran back to the window as quickly as we could. That was quite quickly indeed.

"Madmen," Radamyntos reproached us, as he helped pull us inside. "I'm stuck here with madmen. Inside and outside."

I was acutely aware of the open window, and considered that a more important topic than these complaints. "Shut up and help me close this up!" I demanded.

My heart thundered in my chest as we fumbled at closing the shutters and jamming them home once more. I could hear the shallow, rapid breaths of the German beside me as he hurried to drive home the faggots that would wedge them shut. Like me, he no doubt feared that the creatures would force their way through the open window before we could secure it. But we had time enough and then some; engaged as they were in feasting upon the owners of the villa, the nearest creatures did not immediately move to approach us.

When the task was done, I turned to the German. I had to address the fact that he had saved my life. "If we survive this night," I said to him, "I will see to it that your name is added to the census."[1]

He bowed his great head and nodded.

"If we survive this night," I repeated, and the shutters began to rattle as the dead reached them at last and sought to break through.

---

[1] Castus here refers to the practice of *manumissio censu*, where a slave was set free by having his name entered onto the roll of citizens by the censor. This was usually done at the request of the slave's owner, but the censor could do it independently as well – or, as in this case, at the request of a prominent citizen or important political or military figure.

SEVEN

For an interminable and excruciating time, there were nearly no further sounds but the moans and rattles of the corpse-dolls and the mutterings and sighs of the slaves. Unwilling to risk further defections or suicidal escapes, I ordered Radamyntos to shepherd the surviving slaves into the smallest *cubiculum*, which had a narrow doorway and a window so small that the iron grille that covered it was not much larger than the palm of a man's hand. I was willing to abandon active defense of the outer doors and the other windows in order to keep the slaves under my eye. From this protected position, we prepared once more to attempt to wait out the night.

At first when the wick of a lamp would crackle, we would jump or start; when the sound of the shaking of the doors and shutters would wax louder, we would hold our breaths. But as the hours passed and our adversaries failed to force entrance and no further disturbances arose among the inmates of the house, our concern grew less and we grew more and more confident of our security. When the sky at last – at last – began to glow in the east as the banquet ended and the chariot prepared to return,[1] we faced the dawn with something that came close to good cheer.

As the light grew from grey to bronze, I weighed in my mind the questions that would come with the morning. The deaths of Rufus and his wife had, at least, simplified my command situation. Had they lived, I would have been forced to make provision for their safety; after having sheltered here, I could not have simply abandoned citizens of their class. My return to the encampment would have been complicated by the need to escort them as they moved in the open. It was very likely that they would have insisted on moving the surviving members of their household as well. Their deaths meant that I could leave the household behind – other

[1] This cryptic comment is believed to be a reference to a legend involving the gods Mithras and Helios. These two gods are often represented in contemporary art as banqueting together and then journeying in the latter's sun-chariot. The emperor Commodus, who would have received this letter, is recorded to have been an initiate of the Mithraic mysteries. Mithraism began its rapid spread through the western legions at about this time, so Castus may have been an initiate as well; if so, the striking thing is that faced with supernatural terrors Castus does not appeal to Mithras for aid at any point.

than the German, who I was now determined to extract – and this gained us an important tactical advantage: we could travel across open country, which I judged to be safer than the road. As far as we had seen, these creatures found their victims by sight and sound, like beasts of prey; we could better conceal ourselves at need in open country than exposed on the roadway. Leaving the remaining slaves to their fate meant that they would almost certainly be overcome and slain, and would swell the ranks of the walking dead, but I judged that a rapid return to the base was a priority next to which a few more or less of the creatures was no matter. If the curse were to fail with the full rising of the sun, or if the power of the druid was limited to the span of the festival first mentioned to me by Rufus, all of these questions would of course be rendered moot; but I was not counting on deliverance by the calendar or by a *deus ex machina*[1] – not after all that I had seen.

I decided to reveal my plans to the slaves, to allow them to become accustomed to the idea before it was thrust upon them. I advised them to remain behind the barricades after our departure. "Fortune may call the cursed

[1] Literally "the god in the machine". This expression, coined by Horace, refers to the practice often used in Greek tragedies of lowering a god on to the stage by crane to resolve the plot.

ones to follow us, to try to bring us down under their jaws, and thus leave you in safety. If not, I would counsel you to stay within the house for as long as you can. We will clear the district[1] of these scum soon enough."

Their faces fell, and they trembled as they considered our prospects once they departed. But they had no desire to dispute the issue with us. They had seen how poorly willfulness had served their masters.

All at once the continual rattling at the door stopped. It had filled our ears for so many hours that we had ceased to be aware of it, but this sudden absence was a bracing shock. It hit us like a bucket of cold waste cast from the upper storey of an *insula*.[2]

---

[1] Castus here employs the Latin term "*territorium*". This term was sometimes used to refer to the rural area under the administrative control of a city or *orbs*, and sometimes used to refer to the entire administrative area subject to an individual military leader's political jurisdiction. Both meanings would entail a quite large geographical area, and this may indicate that Castus is anticipating that the effects of the curse have spread quite wide by this point in the tale.

[2] *Insulae* were multi-floor apartment dwellings common in Rome and a few other large cities of the period. Only a few *insula* possessed water or plumbing systems, and those were only effective on the first floor. The poorer tenants on the upper floors would often simply throw their waste out the windows on to the streets below – which made walking on some Roman streets an adventure in itself.

I wondered if my hope that the curse might fail with the arrival of the morning had come to pass, or if some new horror was upon us. I motioned to the others to keep still, and with some hesitation and uncertainly I approached the door. As I drew near to the doorway, I heard the ring of steel from the other side, and was sure I heard the voices of men – true speech and shouts, and not the base rasps and moans of the dead. At once, I turned back the bolts and threw open the door, knowing what I would see on the other side.

Through the open door streamed bright and cheerful morning sunlight. The villa farm, so narrow and forbidding through the long night, spread out before me, its autumn fields open and easily mastered. I saw the reason that the fruitless and interminable assault on the door had been abandoned on the track between the villa and the road. Dismounted horsemen, armed in the Sarmatian manner, advanced down the lane at a walk, cutting the creatures down as they approached. I stepped outside the door, and laughed triumphantly at this unlooked-for relief.

Radamyntos burst out the door and strode by me, shaking his fist at his countrymen. “Right, you bastards!” he yelled. “That’s the way to do it!”

I urged him back behind me, into the space between the door and myself. With rescue so close, I did not want him to rush forward heedlessly, and expose himself to attack in isolation. "Watch," I told him, as the Iazyges arranged themselves into a square, and took their ease while the creatures struggled up to them piecemeal. "See anything that looks familiar?"

The square the men had formed was several men deep. The men on the inside of the square had passed their shields forward, and the men in the front rank laid those shields down on the ground on the four sides of the formation, so that each front ranker would retain his own shield in his hand, while having one or more shields at his feet. When the creatures drew near, their steps on to the grounded shields would be clumsy and slow, as all their movements were clumsy and slow. They almost always stumbled, and the front rankers would strike great blows at them as they struggled to rise.

"Like the river..." Radamyntos replied. "Like the river!"[1] He then shouted out to his

---

[1] Cassius Dio's *Roman History* (Book 72) recounts an episode during the Balkan wars of Marcus Aurelius where a small force of Roman legionary infantry defeated a much larger force of mounted Iazyges in an engagement fought on the ice of a frozen Danube River by employing a similar tactic. It has previously been theorized that it is possible that Castus was the unnamed officer in charge of the Roman force described in Dio's account. The fact that Castus later is put in command of

comrades once again. "You lot aren't as stupid as you look! You actually can learn a trick once in a while!"

After a brief interval, the creatures were all dispatched. In daylight, they were much less intimidating than they had been in the dark of night. They were not much of a threat at all, as long as a sufficient force was brought against them. If they could not greatly outnumber their victims, they were easily overborne. I had great concern for what they could still do to unarmed peasants and tenants at scattered farms, and what they might do if loosed within a city, but I had very little fear for my men.

I did not note the figures of Rufus or his wife among the many *lemures* destroyed by the square, though I kept an eye for them. If they had been taken by the curse like the unlucky Pacilus or Florus, they had not, it seemed, remained to try to force their way back into their home. Two large white Molossians, however, danced up and down the lane, barking at the Iazyges and sniffing at the dead. These I took to be the dogs Rufus had told me about, arriving back at home too late to be useful. The

---

a large detachment of cavalry from this same tribe seems to support this possibility; barbarian forces often were more easily led when placed under officers who had earned their respect in battle. This exchange supports the unofficial designation of Castus as the unknown officer in Dio.

shepherds the dogs had served were probably stalking the fields as corpse-puppets somewhere even now, if they were not among the hapless creatures now lying hacked to pieces in the grass and among the wagon-ruts.

The square broke up and the troopers resumed their advance to the villa. When they drew close I began to pick out individual faces. The detachment was led by Inarmazos, whom I recognized quite easily. I had known him even longer than I had known Radamyntos. He was a strong, stout fellow with a face covered in scars – just the sort of man to have around on such a morning.

"What news, Inarmazos?" I hailed him.

"*Dux*," he saluted me, a little sloppily. Fatigue from a night that no doubt matched ours was apparent in his ragged motions. "We...amazed...you alive." Despite his long service, his camp-Latin was much more broken than that of Radamyntos. Sometimes the toughest ones never quite tame their own tongues. "You not come back, and the groaning ones come to camp instead..."

I could easily imagine what they had thought. "How is the camp?"

"Good, good," he nodded. "The enemy...stupid. Not mass at gate, but walk up to...pit and palisade...stand there, get killed." He shrugged. "If killed right word."

"What new deployments have been made?"

"The camp followers were brought inside the palisade. Our turma and supporting light cavalry were ordered to search the road for you, through this position." Inarmazos was more fluent when discussing specific operations, and his speech could slide into ruts in the road. "All patrols were withdrawn and market parties cancelled."

The actions taken by Decimus Valerius while in temporary command were commendable. Consolidation of forces was the appropriate response to an unknown and novel threat in the absence of the overall commander. The force put at risk to search for me was acceptably small. I would like to officially note the excellent performance of the tribune Decimus Valerius under these trying circumstances.[1]

"Where are the light cavalry you spoke of?" I inquired.

---

[1] As noted earlier, Castus had to be aware of the fact that his absence from the camp, on a social call, during this emergency, could reflect poorly on his command abilities. He may have hoped to deflect attention from his questionable action by lavishing praise on the subordinate who assumed command in his stead. While several of the figures named in this letter are known to us, Decimus Valerius is completely obscure other than this reference.

"Scouting the road ahead. With orders to observe, but not to engage unless necessary. They should return very soon."

This was to our advantage. While we awaited the return of the scouts I considered how best to proceed.

EIGHT

The scouts arrived back at the villa, coming down the track in a rush of brown leaves thrown up by their mounts. To our great felicity they brought with them my own horse and that of Radamyntos, which they had recovered during the night.

Their report was what I expected: the dead were on the road, in decreasing numbers as one proceeded to the east. They attacked anyone who they came across, and were not put off by displays of force. They moved slowly, and had no chance of catching up to a horse, or even a running man – but this did not discourage them from pursuing both. All of this, of course, they related in a jumble of allusions to nameless phantoms of the deserts and mountains of their homeland;[1] it took me some

[1] Except for a few dismissive references in Christian apologia, we have little information about the religion of the Mauri, and no way therefore to identify the myths to which Castus refers here.

pains to distinguish genuine reports of what they had seen from the echoes of the cradle-stories of the Mauri[1] that had no doubt filled their ears all through the night.

I gave the scouts new orders, and put them into service as messengers. I commanded them to ride with all possible speed along the road to bring news to the forces I had ordered back to Lutetia. They were in my name to order those forces to double back and return in two columns, one along the roadway and one through the mixed forest and open country to the north. They were in this way to cover as much terrain as possible on the north bank of the river, sweeping up and putting down the *lemures* as they came, taking care that none should escape to threaten the more populous lands to the east and northeast. Although I had no passports to give them, I ordered the scouts to seize all that they might need, on my authority, from the *mansiones* and *mutationes*[2] they passed along the way, and to compel the soldiery there to join them. They also were to drive before them any travelers they found, as

[1] Although it was well known that the ancestors of the Berbers had served the Romans as light cavalry for centuries, the geographic extent of their service was not well documented. This is the best reference we have to the presence of Mauri cavalry on the northern frontier.
[2] Official way stations maintained by the Roman state, for people and for vehicles and animals respectively.

well as any they might find at the inns, along with any prostitutes or rogues who were there; any who refused to flee the advance of the *lemures* they were to slay, taking care to separate their heads from their bodies before leaving them behind. Any defiant wayfarers they left in their wake would feed the growth of the army of the dead, just as fat peasant granaries would have fed an advancing army of the living; that left us with no choice but to slay those who would not leave, exactly as one would burn the granaries to deny them to the enemy.

These were difficult orders for auxiliary troops, and I knew I asking a great deal of these men. For a provincial, entering an official station with no passport and with a story only a madman or a witch would concoct was a frightening prospect. I was sure most of them would rather stay here among the terror of the dead instead. I dispatched them nonetheless; the task of pacification before me here required all the forces that could be gathered.

The Iazyges I had bring up and water their animals. Once remounted, they were to accompany me back to the camp. I insisted that a horse be found for the German, as well; even though he was as little accustomed to riding as any slave might be, he made his way with us as best he could.

We laughed among ourselves on the road, as men will when they ride away from some skirmish they have lately survived. Under the bronze sunlight the black woods from which the first monsters had sprung upon us were now dappled in the red and gold color common to the season in this district of Gaul. Cleaved and broken bodies still littered the road near where the unlucky Florus had been taken, but other than that grotesque tableau there was little evidence of the night's horrors to be seen. Even the poor huts of the tenants of Rufus were scarcely disturbed, although the tenants were notably now absent.

The good cheer of the morning darkened somewhat as we approached the hill of crosses by the thirteenth milestone. Even the rays of the run itself sickened and became pallid as the bulk of the hill reared up before us. Despite my haste to return to camp, I wanted to examine the bodies we had left to rot on their crosses, to see if any knowledge could be gleaned from them. The Iazyges – wise men – had avoided the hill as they passed it during the night, and could provide not provide me with any report.

The hillside should have been as grim and still as a tomb on the roadside[1] in winter,

---

[1] Roman custom prohibited burial within a city boundary, and this caused tombs to be built on the sides of the roads on the approaches to a city. The roads

but it instead writhed like a mound of carrion covered in maggots. The crucified dead had awakened along with the buried dead and the newly slain. They struggled to be free of the ropes and spikes that bound them to the *pali.* Their broken legs twisted in impossible directions beneath them against the wood. Since they were not restricted in their movements by the pains that living men would have suffered on the cross, one or two of them had even managed to pull a hand free; one had freed his arm by leaving his hand behind with the spike. Their moans rang over our heads like the song of a flock of monstrous birds.

The old man had not been spared by his own curse. His corpse danced on the cross, jerked about by the strings held by the *lemures*, like all the rest. I suspected that the old man's corpse might be a focus of the god's power, and that even though the morning had not banished the curse, disposing of the old man once more might do so. I ordered Inarmazos to see to him. The position of the old man on the cross made this awkward, and Inarmazos did not strike true all at once; but after a few false strikes of the *contus* into the old man's side and chest Inarmazos was able to strike him cleanly through the windpipe, and with a twist of the spear was able to lift the old man's head off his

---

outside Rome in particular were lined with tombs for a considerable distance.

neck. He strode along the hillside holding the head aloft like a bloody standard or eagle. I smiled sadly, thinking of Pacilus – who certainly would have quoted Euripides for us at such a sight.[1]

We watched and waited expectantly for some moments. I do not know what we expected to see, but we did not see it. There was no flash of lightning, no unearthly cries as *lemures* were driven from the bodies of their hapless victims, no jeweled smoke as the god returned to the heavens. There was simply nothing. The destruction of the old man had no effect on the others; the dead on their crosses continued to struggle and moan. Whatever the old man had unleashed was greater than him, and survived him. Another small hope left me, and we descended the hill once more and returned to the road.

---

[1] This recalls the climax of Euripides' *Bacchae*, where the head of Pentheus is proudly displayed as a trophy by Agave.

NINE

The camp was a square that had been laid out on gently sloping land south of the road. The space here between the road and the river was so narrow that the camp very nearly filled it. Originally it had been built for a much larger force that included the units the scouts were now trying to recall. So many gaps had been opened in the line of tribune tents along the *via principalis*[1] and in the blocks of *conturbernia*[2] tents in the sections given over to the centuries when I had divided our forces that on my departure the morning before the camp had looked like the pate of a balding man. But balding man or not, I longed for a sight of it that morning the way one would long for the beautiful face of a lover.

---

[1] One of the two main roads in a Roman camp, running between the two side-gates and in front of the general's tent.

[2] A unit of eight men, roughly the equivalent of a squad, who lived together as a unit.

We made our way all the way to the tenth milestone without challenge or disturbance. The Iazyges and the scouts had cleared the road of the dead quite effectively as they had searched for me through the night. I knew the features of the local country well now, having spent some days in the vicinity. When we passed through a narrow neck of open land between two folds of wood that came close to the road, I knew that once we cleared the trees the camp would be visible on the left. My heart rose as we covered the last few *stadia*. But even we rode through the gap and as the tree line withdrew towards the river on our left, I could tell that something was wrong.

Based on the report I had received from Inarmazos, I knew that the *lemures* had attacked the camp during the night – but he had described the attacks as coming piecemeal, with the monsters attacking the palisade one or two at a time. I expected to see the dead in the open area around the camp, and even anticipated that we might be forced to fight some small number of them as we made our way to the gate. But as the camp first came into view, my immediate impression was of far too much movement outside the palisade, concentrated much too heavily near the *porta praetoria*.[1] At this distance my eyes strained to pick out

[1] The main gate of the camp.

individual figures, and to determine the overall tactical situation.

Radamyntos and Inarmazos, being younger men, were somewhat sharper-sighted than me. They could already see what was happening, and what they saw shocked them into action; without orders, they heeled their horses forward sharply, dashing toward the gate. The remaining troopers could not resist the impulse to join the charge of the decurions and were swept forward as well. I was ignored when I shouted for them to stop.[1] With no other other alternative, I spurred my horse to follow them.

As we drew closer I could see the gate more clearly. The *lemures* there were thick as the fallen leaves upon the road. I quickly counted tens,[2] and estimated at least two hundred of the corpse-puppets outside the gate. Even more alarmingly, the gate was open, and there was a struggle inside the camp. A few of the

---

[1] Despite their extensive service in multiple theatres of operations the Sarmatians were still barbarian auxiliaries at the end of the day, and their reliability and discipline were always in question, particularly among the cavalry. It is notable that Castus does not even dwell upon this breach of discipline and takes it as a matter of course.

[2] A Roman officer would be trained in the art of rapidly determining the size of an enemy force based on the total ground area it took up and the density of the enemy's formation.

dead looked to be the original rebels, who could be identified by the mud of their brief burial that still marked them. A larger number, seemingly folk of the countryside, were marred by the wounds wrought by an attack of the creatures – terrible bites to the face, limbs or extremities gnawed and torn away. And some of the dead – too many, enough to make my blood run cold – bore the arms and armor of my own men.

The Iazyges charged into the rear of the creatures in front of the gate like a giant steel hammer striking an anvil made of limp flesh. The monsters closest to them crumpled into a mass of tangled and broken limbs. The horses trampled many; others were skewered like sausages on the long Sarmatian spears.

But the power of the charge was quickly blunted.

One of the most powerful weapons brought to bear by cavalry is the fear it strikes into the heart of the enemy; and here was a foe without the wit to feel fear. A force of living men caught in the rear by such a charge would have instantly broken and fled; the force we faced would not break, but had to be utterly destroyed. And the charge of the Iazyges was ill suited to such a task. Spear strikes did not deliver the type of wound needed to destroy one of the monsters. Trampling might crush an arm or break a leg or the back – but the gnawing horrors then merely crawled, and continued to attack. The horses, steady enough during the charge, began to panic as the crushed and shattered monsters writhed like maggots under their hooves. I saw one horse stumble and spill its rider; the *lemures* pulled down another and swarmed over him as he screamed to his fellows for aid. Even armored as they were, with no momentum the troopers were vulnerable; the longer they floundered in a disordered melee, the worse their predicament would become.

I slid from my horse roughly, almost losing my footing in my haste to dismount. The German appeared beside me; he had enough sense to know that he was no cavalryman, and had made his approach to the gate on foot. "We've got to pull them out!" I shouted, as much to myself as to him.

Waving my sword in the air, I cried out, "A line! A line!" again and again, in a voice pitched high to be heard above the clamor of the fight. I ran to and fro amid those Iazyges who had been near the back of the *turmae* and were still unengaged, pushing and urging them back. One or two heeded me and dismounted; others saw their example, and joined them. Slowly a short line took shape. The German danced around the outskirts of the mass of fighters like a forum clown, leaping into the air and clapping his hands over his head;

whenever he got the attention of one of our men through this device, he frantically pointed to me and to the line. And in this way, bit by bit, we pulled the troopers out, and got them into a sword line.

As more and more troopers extracted themselves and joined the line, those who remained behind found themselves more and more outnumbered by the creatures. Those who had led the charge were naturally left worst off of all. I cursed as I saw Inarmazos pulled down. He disappeared beneath a pile of bodies, slashing with his sword the whole time. He rose once, but was borne down again quickly. Radamyntos was more fortunate. He was fighting his way back to the line on foot, when I saw him reverse direction and push his way out of the melee on the other edge, just to the north of the gate; he had no doubt seen that he could reach safety more easily on that side than he could by trying to retreat the way he came.

The struggle went on for some time, but more profitably once some order had been made. Our comrades fought their way out the gate, and the monsters were caught between our line and their advance like olives between the basin and the grinding-stones.[1] The hardest

[1] Before being pressed for oil, olives would be passed through a mill-like device that ground them into a mash and removed their seed pits.

to put down were those legionaries who had fallen and joined with the cursed dead. Many of them still wore helmets and armor that provided good protection against attacks directed at the head and neck. I notched the sword of Rufus against the neck plate of a bloodless infantryman; the shock of it nearly broke my wrist. My next strike caught metal as well, and the blade broke near the shoulders. Deprived of a weapon, I withdrew behind the line, and watched the remainder of the fight. I cannot say that I commanded, for the destruction of the rest of the corpse-puppets was mere butchery that required only encouragement and not direction.

When the men from the camp reached our line I saw that Decimus Valerius had led them out in person. I hailed him, and praised him for his courage. He had a fire burning in his eyes that did not fade even now that the fight was won. As I walked with him back to the gate, he related how the camp, so secure the night before when the scouts had been dispatched, had erupted into chaos less than an hour ago with the sudden appearance of large numbers of the creatures inside the gate. Not knowing that the bites of the monsters imparted cursed and fatal wounds, Valerius had brought many lightly wounded men inside the palisade, and the story of Pacilus had played itself out scores of times over. I could not blame him for this; the fate of Pacilus had caught me not only unawares but half asleep.

TEN

The vermin had all been cleared away from the gate, but small knots of them still lingered, moaning and snarling, here and there in the cleared space between the camp and the road. With Decimus Valerius and a handful of men I moved to the east of the gate, to oversee the reduction of the enemy that remained. The German tagged along, and none of the legionaries attempted to prevent it; his battlefield promotion, as it were, from slave to client was obvious enough for them to readily see. Radamyntos had headed in this direction when he had fought his way out of the horde, as well, and I wanted to see how my companion of the long night and morning had fared.

The east side of the camp was where the Iazyges had set up their shrine to Mars.[1] The

[1] The Romans tended to interpret any foreign worship with military overtones as a variation on their own worship of Mars. What we know of the Sarmatian

aedes[1] was not acceptable for this purpose, since the Mars of their country wears a strange aspect, due to his many intrigues with the barbarian gods there. The other soldiers suffered them this use of the sacred space held in common outside the palisade as a sign of respect for their bravery and skill. The shrine was a simple circle in the grass marked out with white stones, in the center of which a sword was driven straight down into the earth so that only its handle was visible. Many of the *lemures* had gathered there, tempted I suppose by the opportunity for sacrilege and defilement.

Many bodies had been hacked to pieces here. They lay in pieces on the ground in a circle around the sword handle, like the petals of a flower. Three of the dismounted troopers from my line had dashed to the little shrine as soon as the pressure at the gate was relieved, and they had attacked the creatures there in an outraged frenzy. Their anger at the shrine's violation had not relented even now, and they continued to attack those wretched ones still left in the general vicinity. We moved up so that the men with Decimus Valerius could support them, and grimly stepped through the gore-drenched flower. Before we could make it

---

sword-cult would link it more closely with the worship of Apollo than that of Mars.

[1] The *aedes* was a small shrine set up in the middle of a Roman camp to hold the legionary standards.

across, a glint of gold caught my eye amid the ruined bodies on the ground. I passed it by, but somehow the shape of it drew my attention back. I stopped and turned around to see it better, and the jeweled eye of a golden hedgehog stared up at me from the belt of a headless corpse. I examined the ground all around, and nearby I found the head of Radamyntos, recognizable despite the many bites and scratches it bore.

I could easily see what had befallen him: After he freed himself from the melee, he had seen the corpse-puppets violating the border of the shrine. In a rage, he had charged into his enemies in the same frenzy that seized his countrymen even now. Dehorsed at some point, he had taken many of the cursed wounds as he fought the creatures alone. Some unwounded man who happened across the scene, in order to prevent the *lemures* from seizing another victim, had taken his head. Knowing Radamyntos, the man who had taken his head had in all likelihood done so at the decurion's own request.

A profound anger swept me as I stood there in the blood-soaked grass. All in a moment and without words I saw how Radamyntos, who had scoffed at the way Rufus had been abandoned by Christus, had been brought low by his own piety. I saw how the old druid had laid me low with his curse, but how this had left him hanging on a cross just the same. And I felt, deep in a place where the voice does not come from or reach, how we are all helpless before the gods, who succor or destroy us in their own time and by their own mind. And in that moment some facet of my heart threw itself over to that caprice of the gods and embraced it. I do not know if my anger was entirely my own, or if the Sarmatian Mars entered into me and filled me with divine madness.[1] Since I was without a weapon, I reached down and seized the earth-bound sword. It came out of the ground easily, like a loose sapling or a withered vine. I waved it over my head to shake free the clods of dirt that stuck to the blade. I did not know a great deal about the cult of the Sarmatian Mars, but I knew that removing the sword from its place without leave and outside of ritual had to be a great sacrilege; that I did so nonetheless is one reason I believe that I must have been taken by the god.

The power of the god swept through me like fire through the dry thickets of the mountains; foam arose from my mouth, and I could feel my eyes gleam beneath my brows. A dark cloud covered the sun and the bright morning was plunged into gray. I waved the sword again and shouted, though I could not

---

[1] *Enthousiasmos*, one of the few Greek terms Castus employs without attempting to substitute with Latin.

summon any words. The dark cloud broke into sudden rain, and my thought was extinguished.[1]

[1] This description of the battle-madness of Castus is a Latin mongrelization of lines from the *Iliad* containing Homer's description of a similar madness that swept over Hector.

ELEVEN

After that, my memory fails. I know that I started to run, but can remember nothing else. My next recollection is of sitting the mud on the ground outside the *praetorium*,[1] with the sword of the god at my feet, as the drops of a light rain fell on my face. Shafts of sunlight pierced through the rain clouds in the distance, and the shadows were scattered and light returned to my mind. I saw what I ought to see: the sky and the earth and the camp about me; the blindness of furor was lifted.[2]

A score or more of my men were about me, but few of them would look in my direction or meet my eyes. Most of them stamped and

---

[1] The general's command tent, located at the center of the camp.

[2] The opening of this chapter recalls both the description of the madness of Turnus in Virgil's *Aeneid* and Euripides' description of a psychotic episode suffered by Herakles. Together with the Homeric reference at the end of the last chapter, these are the strongest evidence that *De Bello Lemures* was in fact a literary exercise.

shuffled nervously, and pretended to be distracted by sights in the distance. Decimus Valerius was there, and he at least spoke to me – perhaps because his courage was greater, or perhaps because he thought his rank left him no choice.

"*Dux*!" he called to me, as one would call to one in a feverish sleep. "It is over! It has ended!"

"Has it?"

When I stood up, I discovered that the mud about my feet was not the result of the rain alone. Blood and gore dripped from my tunic, armor and cloak. It had been churned into the wet earth below me until all was a red muck. I paid it no mind; I knew it was not my own.

"The camp is secure," Decimus Valerius said. "The enemy here is destroyed."

"Yes. Here." Outside the ditch and wall there were only the green fields, the wood, the river, and the road. After a pause, I decided that I had to ask him the question that was foremost in my mind. "What did I do?"

Even those few who could bear to look at me now turned their heads. "I did not see," he lied. "The slave brought you in." He pointed to the German, who crouched between the sentries by the tent-flap, hiding his head from the rain beneath a *sagum*. "Perhaps he saw."

The German looked up, and the glazed-over fear and weariness there told me that he had seen, but that it would be too brutal to question him. He stood up and walked over to me, and knelt and picked the sword out of the red mud. The muttering this engendered was cut off into silence when he handed the weapon to me. Calling for attendants, I turned away from the crowd of men and carried the sword into my tent.

After the stains upon me had been washed away into many basins of clear river water, I allowed my officers into the tent. The men were very tired, but it was important to issue certain orders immediately. At all costs the *lemures* must be prevented from reaching the port, and the thickly settled district in its lee. The clamor of the battle around the camp had drawn the monsters to it, and I trusted to Fortune that none of them had yet passed the camp by and brought their curse to the city. I dispatched five centuries under Decimus Valerius to hold the road between the camp and Oceanus. Another four centuries I sent to hold the two possible river crossings. If we could keep the creatures north of the river and east of the town, when our reinforcements approached they could drive the enemy north into the dense wood, where there were few farms and few men for them to feed upon to swell their numbers. If this could be achieved we could have hope that the curse could be contained and then destroyed.

The balance of my men such as could be spared from the duty of guarding the walls of the camp I ordered to rest. Some of them I will send to Rome by the fastest way, to bring you this letter. For no matter how Fortune smiles upon our plans here, should even a single one of these creatures make its way out of our net, the entire province is threatened, and the Empire itself. I must make to you the greatest warning that can be made. I know the many demands that command places upon you, but no threat that we face on the frontier subjects us to as much jeopardy as the threat we face here. I beg for as many troops as can be spared, to scour the land south and east of my position, to be sure no *lemur*[1] stalks the land there.

I remain your humble servant.

The text here ends. Cassius Dio and Herodian both record that at about this time the Emperor Commodus received a "warning" brought to him by "javelin-men" sent by "the lieutenants of Britain". The force dispatched by Castus described here would seem to be a

---

[1] Castus on multiple occasions employs a singular form of the word *lemures*, which was previously believed to only exist in the plural form. This may simply be a usage error on Castus' part.

good candidate to be the bearers of this warning. However, both historians record that the substance of the warning dealt with the assassination plot of Perennis, and neither gives any inkling of any more bizarre or grave tale associated with that incident. Barring the discovery of definitive archaeological evidence or additional lost documentation, the story of the resolution of Castus' strange tale may forever elude us.

Made in the USA
Las Vegas, NV
30 June 2021

25723424R00066